Stillwater

A Perfect Fit

Adapted by Meredith Rusu from the teleplay, "A Perfect Fit," by Craig Lewis

From the Apple TV+ series developed by Rob Hoegee, produced by Gaumont, and based on the Scholastic book series by Jon J Muth

ISBN 978-1-338-80577-2
10 9 8 7 6 5 4 3 2   22 23 24 25 26
Printed in the U.S.A. 40
First printing 2022
Book design by Robin Hoffmann

Scholastic Inc.

ONE DAY, Addy, Michael, and Karl were in the backyard building a soapbox race car. The big race was in just a few days, and they wanted their car to go faster than fast!

They each had an important job to do.
Michael was drawing the plans.
Addy was building the car.
And Karl . . . well, Karl was still figuring out what his important job would be.

"Can I help you draw?" Karl asked Michael. "I'm good
at using rulers."

"Thanks, but . . . it's kind of a one-person job,"
Michael said. "Why don't you see if Addy needs help?"

"Oh, okay," said Karl.

Karl went over to where Addy was working. "Can I help you build?" he asked.
"It's kind of tricky," Addy told him. "I still need to fix a few things."

"I could put the wheels on!" Karl offered.

Addy shook her head. "It's not ready for the wheels yet."

"Oh, okay," said Karl.

Just then Stillwater came into the backyard with a warm smile. "I thought the builders could use a lemonade break," he said. "How is the car coming along?"

"I'm triple-checking all my measurements!" Michael said proudly.

"And I'm getting the steering just right," said Addy.

Karl looked down at his lemonade.

"What about you, Karl?" asked Stillwater. "Are you having fun?"

"Um, I don't know," said Karl.

Stillwater chuckled. "I usually know whether or not I'm having fun. Why don't you take a walk with me and we can talk about it?"

Karl sighed as he walked beside Stillwater. "I want to help build the soapbox car," he said. "But I can't draw plans like Michael. And I can't build like Addy. It's like they don't need me. I'm useless."

"Useless?" asked Stillwater. "I thought your name
was Karl."

Karl couldn't help giggling. Stillwater had a way of
making the children feel better.

"We all have gifts to share," Stillwater told him.
"Sometimes, we have to look a little closer to find them.
Would you like to hear a story?"

Stillwater began . . .

Hannah lived in a house on a hill.
Every morning, she gathered her two
large pots to collect the day's water.

One pot was happy because it never spilled a single drop.

But the other pot was sad. She had a large crack in her side, and she spilled all her drops on the long journey home.

"What troubles you, my friend?" Hannah asked when she saw how sad the pot was.

"It's this crack in my side," the pot said. "Every day, you fill two pots but only return with one pot's worth of water. And a pot with a hole is a useless pot."

Hannah shook her head. "I chose you because of that hole in your side. Perhaps you will understand why if you take a closer look at the path on our way home."

The pot did just that, and she was surprised by what she found.

Her side of the path bloomed with lovely, colorful flowers!
"Where did they all come from?" she asked.

"They came from you!" Hannah replied. "I planted seeds on your side of the path. Every day, drips from the hole in your side have watered them. Look what beauty you have brought to our world! A pot with a hole is a very special pot, with a very special gift to give."

"Hannah knew her pot was special all along."
Stillwater finished his story. "Sometimes, we all
need help seeing how special we are."

"And speaking of needing help . . ." Stillwater
pointed to his lemon tree. "It seems I've picked
all the lemons I can easily reach. My paws are
too big to get the ones near the trunk."

"I can help!" Karl exclaimed. "I'm small enough to get in there and reach them."

Karl easily climbed up into the middle of the tree, where all the lemons were.

"That was a perfect job for you," said Stillwater.

"Yeah!" said Karl. "I wonder if there might be a perfect job for me building the soapbox car, too. I'd better go and see."

Karl hurried back to Addy and Michael. But he was surprised to find they were already finished building the car! "You're done?" he asked, disappointed.

"Not exactly," said Michael. "We built the car too small. I don't think we can race it."

Addy looked at Karl. Her eyes lit up. "It may be too small for us to race," she realized. "But I bet Karl could fit!"

Karl eagerly leapt into the driver's seat . . . and he was just the right size!

"Look, Stillwater!" Karl said as they got
ready to race. "I found the perfect job after all!"
  "You certainly did." Stillwater smiled. "A job
that I would call a perfect fit."